BURIED TREASURE!

Frank looked over at Chet. He was crouched down in the same spot, still with his back to the rest of the kids. It looked as if he was tugging at something on the ground.

What is he doing? Frank wandered closer.

Chet heard him coming and looked around. "Hey, Frank, help me!" he said eagerly.

"Help you with what?" Frank hurried over.

Chet tugged again at something. Frank could see it now. It looked like the edge of a piece of thin yellow paper buried in the dirt.

"I was following some raccoon tracks over here," Chet said. "But I think I just found a treasure map!"

THE HARDY BOYS®

SECRET FILES #3

Mystery Map

BY **FRANKLIN W. DIXON**

ILLUSTRATED BY **SCOTT BURROUGHS**

ALADDIN • NEW YORK LONDON TORONTO SYDNEY

This book is a work of fiction. Any references to historical events, real people, or real locales are used fictitiously. Other names, characters, places, and incidents are the product of the author's imagination, and any resemblance to actual events or locales or persons, living or dead, is entirely coincidental.

ALADDIN

An imprint of Simon & Schuster Children's Publishing Division
1230 Avenue of the Americas, New York, NY 10020
First Aladdin paperback edition August 2010
Text copyright © 2010 by Simon & Schuster, Inc.
Illustrations copyright © 2010 by Scott Burroughs
All rights reserved, including the right of reproduction in whole or in part in any form.
ALADDIN is a trademark of Simon & Schuster, Inc., and related logo is a registered trademark of Simon & Schuster, Inc.
THE HARDY BOYS is a registered trademark of Simon & Schuster, Inc.
For information about special discounts for bulk purchases, please contact Simon & Schuster Special Sales at 1-866-506-1949 or business@simonandschuster.com.
The Simon & Schuster Speakers Bureau can bring authors to your live event. For more information or to book an event contact the Simon & Schuster Speakers Bureau at 1-866-248-3049 or visit our website at www.simonspeakers.com.
Designed by Lisa Vega
The text of this book was set in Garamond.
Manufactured in the United States of America/1214 OFF
10 9 8 7
Library of Congress Control Number 2009937537
ISBN 978-1-4169-9165-6
ISBN 978-1-4424-0719-0 (eBook)

CONTENTS

1

Dodgeball Danger

"Gotcha!" someone yelled.

Frank Hardy spun around. A ball was flying toward him. He ducked just in time. "Missed me!" he yelled back.

Then he swooped down and picked up another ball off the ground. There were at least ten people in the dodgeball game. And about eight balls. That made things extra exciting.

One of the other players was Frank's brother, Joe. He was chasing their friend Iola Morton with

one of the balls. But they were both too far away
for Frank to try to hit them.

Frank looked around for someone else. His
friend Phil Cohen was nearby. He was leaning over

to pick up a ball. Frank grinned and winged his ball at Phil.

"You're out!" he called as the ball bounced off Phil's back.

"Aw, man!" Phil complained. "You got me out last time too, Frank!"

"I'll get him back for you, Phil," Joe called out. He dashed over and flung the ball he was holding at Frank.

Frank dodged it easily. Joe was pretty good at dodgeball. But sometimes he got too excited and impatient to aim carefully enough.

"You'll have to do better than that," Frank said. "Or—"

ZZZZZZZIP!

A ball whizzed past, inches in front of his nose. It was going really, really fast. It almost hit Phil in the head, but he ducked just in time.

"Ha!" someone shouted.

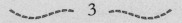

Frank spun around. Adam Ackerman was standing at the edge of the game. Adam was the worst bully in Bayport. He was eight years old, just like Joe, which made him a whole year younger than Frank, Phil, and some of the others. But he was bigger than all of them—and a lot meaner. He was always getting in trouble at school for picking fights and stealing kids' lunches.

"Hey!" Joe yelled. "Who invited *you* to play?"

"It's a public park, dummy," Adam taunted. "I can be here if I want."

Frank frowned. Adam was right. They were playing in Bayport Park. Everyone was allowed to play games there, or have picnics in the grassy parts, or hike in the woods. But that didn't mean it was right for Adam to butt in on their game.

Adam grabbed a ball off the ground. He had an evil glint in his eye as he looked around for another victim. Then he smiled.

"Great," he muttered gleefully. "Easy target!"

Frank followed Adam's gaze. Uh-oh. He was staring right at Chet Morton.

Chet was Iola's brother and one of the Hardy brothers' best friends. He wasn't very good at dodgeball or most other sports. But he had lots of other interests. His friends and family liked to joke that Chet had a new hobby every week. Lately he was interested in learning how to identify and follow animal tracks. Right now Chet was at the edge of the woods, facing away from the dodgeball game. He was bending over and staring at something on the ground.

Frank groaned. Chet was probably looking for animal tracks or something. When he got caught up in a new hobby, Chet forgot about everything else. That meant he'd never see Adam's attack coming.

Joe and the others saw what Adam was about to do too. "Don't do it, Adam!" Iola cried.

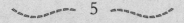

Adam ignored her. He wound up and threw the ball at Chet as hard as he could. And that was pretty hard.

"Noooooo!" Joe howled. Flinging himself forward, he tried to block the ball with his body before it reached Chet.

THUNK! Joe blocked the shot, all right. But not with his body. He accidentally used his face instead.

"Ow!" he cried as the ball slammed him right in the eye. He dropped to his knees and grabbed his face.

"Grow up, Adam!" Iola stomped over to the bully. "In case you're wondering why we never invite you to play, *that's* why!" She pointed to Joe, who was still clutching his face.

"Yeah. Either play by the rules or go away," Phil added. Some of the other kids nodded. Others hung back, looking nervous. Almost everyone was at least a little bit afraid of Adam.

But Joe was too annoyed to be scared. He stood up and hurried over, still rubbing his face. "Adam," he asked, "why do you have to be such a jerk?"

Frank looked over at Chet. He hadn't even noticed his close call. He was crouched down in the same spot, still with his back to the rest of the kids. It looked as if he was tugging at something on the ground.

What is he doing? Frank wandered closer.

Chet heard him coming and looked around. "Hey, Frank, help me!" he said eagerly.

"Help you with what?" Frank hurried over.

Chet tugged again at something. Frank could see it now. It looked like the edge of a piece of thin yellow paper buried in the dirt.

"I was following some raccoon tracks over here," Chet said. "But I think I just found a treasure map!"

2

Trash or Map?

ust go away, Adam!" Iola yelled.

Adam crossed his arms. "Who's going to make me?"

Joe looked around for Frank. He was usually pretty good at calming everyone down at times like this.

But Frank wasn't even paying attention to Adam anymore. He was way over by the edge of the woods with Chet. They were leaning over, looking at something on the ground.

Iola and the others were still busy yelling at Adam. They didn't even notice when Joe left. He jogged over to his brother and Chet.

"What are you guys doing over here?" he asked.

"Chet found something," Frank said.

Chet nodded eagerly. "I'm pretty sure it's a treasure map!"

"A treasure map? Really?" Joe couldn't help being doubtful. Who would hide a treasure map in boring old Bayport? Still, he bent down to help the others dig out the piece of paper. It was pretty muddy after being buried in the ground.

Joe noticed that one corner of the paper was missing and its edges were ragged. "Looks like something chewed off part of it," he said.

Chet nodded. "It could have been that raccoon I was tracking." He pointed to some small, hand-like prints in the mud. "Or maybe a dog or something."

Joe looked over at the sidewalk across the street. He remembered that a tall, blond kid had been walking a lively hound puppy on a leash over there earlier. Joe had noticed them because he loved dogs. He didn't know the kid, but he'd seen him around. He was pretty sure the puppy was new, though. They were both gone now anyway.

"It was probably a dog," Joe said. "They like to

eat anything and everything. That's why Mom says we can't get one."

Frank was carefully spreading out the muddy paper. "Sorry, Chet," he said. "I don't think it's a treasure map after all. Looks like a used wrapper from a fast-food burger."

"Yuck," Joe said. "You're right. I think that's ketchup there under the dirt."

Chet grabbed the burger wrapper and turned it over. "Look," he said, pointing. "There's stuff written on the back. See? It *is* a map!"

Joe leaned forward for a closer look. Just then there was a shout from behind them. Glancing over his shoulder, he saw Adam heading their way.

"Oops," he said, shoving the wrapper at Chet. "Better hide this before Adam sees it. You know how he is."

Chet looked nervous. "You take it," he whispered, shoving it back at Joe.

Joe shrugged and stuffed the wrapper in his pocket. Then he and Frank walked back toward Adam and the others. Chet stayed a little behind them.

"Hiding from me, Morton?" Adam taunted him with a smirk.

"Leave him alone," Frank said.

Just then there was a buzzing sound. Phil reached into his pocket. "It's my phone," he said.

Phil had the fanciest cell phone of anyone his age. He loved gadgets and anything high tech. When he grew up, he wanted to be an inventor.

He answered the phone. Then he held it out to Frank and Joe.

"It's for you two," he said. "It's your mom."

"Thanks." Frank took the phone from him.

"Aw, how cute," Adam goaded Joe, using a baby voice. "Your mommy is checking up on you! Is she afraid her two little babies will get lost trying to find your way home all by your baby selves?"

"No way," Joe answered with a frown. "If someone with a brain as tiny as yours can find your way home, we can do it too."

Adam just smirked. "If you say so, Baby Joe."

Soon Frank hung up and handed the phone back to Phil. "We'd better head home," he told Joe.

"Already?" Joe asked unhappily.

"Just come on," Frank said. "Mom wants us to stop at the grocery store on the way."

"We'll walk you to the store," Chet said. "It's on our way home. Right, Iola?"

He still sounded nervous. That reminded Joe that Adam was still hanging around. As long as he was there, staying at the park wouldn't be much fun anyway.

The four of them said good-bye to the others and walked away. "I still don't see why we had to leave so early," Joe complained. "The store's right across the street. It will only take a second to stop in there."

"I know," Frank said. "But Mom wants us home early. Aunt Gertrude's coming for dinner tomorrow, remember? So we're supposed to help make sure our room is nice and clean."

"Aunt Gertrude?" Iola asked. "Is that your aunt who lives in New York City?"

Joe groaned. "Yeah. I forgot she was coming to visit this weekend."

He loved his Aunt Gertrude, who was his father's sister. And it was fun to travel to New York City to visit her at her apartment. There was always lots to do in her busy neighborhood.

But it wasn't as much fun when she made the trip out to visit them in Bayport. She was always making the boys sit up straight and keep their elbows off the table when they ate. Frank did that anyway, so she was always praising him. But Joe sometimes forgot.

Soon they were at the door of the grocery store.

"What time is your aunt coming?" Chet asked. "Want to meet up at the park again in the morning?"

"Sure. She's not getting here until dinnertime," Joe said.

Frank nodded. "See you tomorrow."

3

Secret Spots

At dinner Joe reached for the napkin on his lap to wipe his mouth. As he did, his hand brushed against something sticking out of his pocket. It was the crumpled yellow paper Chet had dug up.

"Guess what?" Joe told his parents, pulling it out. "Chet found this in the park. He thinks it's a map to hidden treasure."

"That's nice." Mrs. Hardy hardly looked up

from her food. "Don't drop any of that dirt on the floor, please. I just cleaned the rug."

"A treasure map, eh?" Mr. Hardy said. "Well, I suppose you two are just the ones to track down any pirate's booty hidden in Bayport. You can add it to the list of mysteries you've already solved."

"That's true," Joe agreed. The brothers had solved a couple of mysteries around Bayport lately. It turned out that they had a knack for it. Everyone said they were following in their father's footsteps.

"I doubt it's really a treasure map, though," Frank added.

"Hmm." Mrs. Hardy checked her watch. "Would you all excuse me, please? I really need to put the towels in the dryer."

She got up from the table. So did Mr. Hardy. "I'm finished too," he said. "I, er, have some things to do."

They both hurried out of the room in opposite directions. Frank frowned as he watched them go. Then he turned to Joe.

"What's with them?" he asked. "They're acting kind of weird."

"Yeah, I guess." Joe was still looking at the treasure map.

"I hope nothing's wrong," Frank said.

Joe shrugged. "Don't worry so much. Adults act weird sometimes. It's just a fact of life." He pushed the dirty yellow paper across the table. "Check this out. I think Chet's right—it really does look like someone drew a map on here."

Frank took the map and looked at it. "It definitely could be a map," he agreed. "Look— whoever made it drew a bunch of trees here. Think that's supposed to be the woods?"

Joe leaned across the table for a better look. "Probably. And what about this? Looks like a baseball diamond—like the one at the park. So that means the woods are probably the ones right out there."

Joe pointed toward the back of the Hardys' house. A strip of forest lay between their house and the park. There were lots of trails back there

for hikers, mountain bikers, and horseback riders. The brothers cut through there all the time to get to the main part of town from their neighborhood.

"And this blob here is probably the duck pond behind the post office." Frank pointed to another mark on the paper. "So it really does look like a

map of Bayport. But why would someone draw a map of Bayport, unless . . .”

“Unless it really is a map to a hidden treasure!” Joe broke in, sounding excited. “Awesome! That twisty dotted line probably marks the trail to the spot where the treasure is buried.”

Frank peered at the line. “It’s pretty hard to see with all the dirt and stuff,” he said. “Maybe we should show it to Dad. He might have some tips for figuring it out.”

Joe jumped to his feet. “Let’s go find him!”

They hurried out of the dining room. In the kitchen their mother was talking on the phone.

“Yes, Gertrude,” she was saying when they entered. “Fenton will be there to pick you up at the station. I hope you—”

“Mom!” Joe whispered. “Where’s Dad?”

His mother frowned and shook her head. Suddenly, Joe remembered that she hated it when he tried to talk to her while she was on the phone. *Oops,* he thought.

Frank tugged on his arm. "Come on," he murmured. "We can find Dad ourselves."

The next place they looked was the living room. Their dad liked to read the newspaper there after dinner. But there was no sign of him. He wasn't in the den watching TV either, or in his bedroom.

Frank and Joe stopped in the upstairs hallway. "This is turning into a real mystery," Frank joked. "I think we need to investigate."

"Maybe Dad has a secret tree house of his own," Joe said.

Frank grinned. Mr. Hardy had helped the boys build a tree house in the woods out back. Nobody knew it was there except the three of them. Lately it had become the headquarters for the brothers' investigations.

"If we're going to solve the case of the missing father, we'd better do it the right way," Frank said. "The six *W*s, remember?"

"Who, What, When, Where, Why, and How." Joe ticked each word off on his fingers. "Okay, we know the Who."

"We're looking for Dad, that's the Who," Frank agreed. "The What is that he's missing, and the When is right now."

"So all we need to find out is Why and How, and maybe then we'll figure out the Where," Joe said. "I know! Let's check the garage and see if his car is there."

"Great idea," Frank said. "If it is, we'll know he didn't go far."

Soon they were out in the garage. Their parents' cars were parked neatly side by side.

"That means he's probably still in the house

somewhere." Joe glanced out the garage window. "Or maybe the yard."

Frank pointed to several pairs of boots lined up just outside the door leading into the house. "His outside shoes are here," he said. "That means he's probably not working in the garden or anything like that."

Joe glanced up. "Did you hear that thump?" he asked. "I think I just solved the mystery."

"Of course! The spare room!" Frank couldn't believe they'd forgotten to look there. For the past month or more, their father had been fixing up the area over the garage. That was the Where.

The brothers left the garage and hurried around the outside of the house. They started up the steps to the spare room, which started near the kitchen door.

When they reached the landing, they saw that

the spare room door was shut. Joe reached for the handle.

"It's locked," he said.

Frank nodded. "Dad's been secretive about the spare room all along," he recalled. "You decided he was going to surprise us by letting one of us move in there so we could each have our own room, remember?"

"I still think he's going to do that," Joe said. "What else could it—"

Just then the door opened and their father looked out. When he saw them, he quickly stepped out onto the landing and shut the door behind him.

"Yes, boys?" he asked. "What is it?"

"We wanted to ask you about the treasure map," Frank said.

Mr. Hardy checked his watch. "Let's take a look later, all right?" he said. "Right now I should go help your mother."

He hurried down the steps and into the house. Joe watched him go. Then he tested the spare room door.

"Still locked," he reported. "So much for the Why," he said with a frown.

Frank bit his lip. "That was kind of weird," he

said slowly. "It was like Dad didn't want us to catch a glimpse in there."

The two of them stared at each other. Frank knew they were both thinking the same thing.

What was their father trying to hide?

4

The Search Begins

"I still think one of us is getting the spare room," Joe told Frank.

It was the next morning. The two of them were walking through the woods on their way to the park to meet Chet.

"Don't get your hopes up," Frank said. "That spare room is more like a little apartment than a regular bedroom. It even has its own bathroom. Plus, it's totally separate from the rest of the house.

There's no way Mom and Dad would let one of us live out there all alone."

Joe shrugged. He wasn't ready to give up hope. "Then maybe they'll let *both* of us move out there," he said. "That would be cool too. It's a lot bigger than our room now."

"Then what would they do with our old room?" Frank still sounded doubtful.

"Maybe Mom will turn it into that craft room she's always wanted."

"Or maybe the spare room will be her new craft room," Frank said. "That makes more sense. We should probably just ask them."

"I already tried," Joe said. "I asked Dad before breakfast. He just said something about needing more storage space. Then when I asked Mom a few minutes later, she said it was 'up in the air.'"

"Hmm," Frank said. "That is kind of weird."

Joe nodded, feeling excited at the thought of

a bigger, better bedroom. "It has to be almost finished by now. I bet they're just waiting for Aunt Gertrude's visit to be over with before they surprise us."

The boys had come to the edge of the woods. Joe looked around for Chet. It was early, and the park wasn't very crowded yet. There were only a few people on the swings, and there was a small group of teenage girls playing kickball. Joe soon spotted Chet watching the kickball game.

Chet was watching for the Hardys too. He waved and hurried over to them.

"Did you bring the map?" he asked eagerly.

Joe pulled it out of his pocket. "Right here. We think we figured out some of the markings and stuff."

"Cool!" Chet grinned. "Treasure, here we come!"

The three of them bent over the map. "This has to be the playground," Frank told Chet. He pointed to a drawing that looked like a swing set. "And these trees are the woods."

"Right." Joe waved a hand at a section of woods nearby. "The dotted line starts in there, so we should probably go look around for more clues."

Soon the three of them were making their way

down a dirt trail. Chet pushed aside a branch. "Do you think we're going the right way?" he asked.

Frank nodded, checking the map. "The spot where the dotted line starts should be right up ahead."

Joe was in the lead. He hopped over a fallen tree trunk and then glanced back at the others. "What do you think the treasure will be? Could it really be pirate's booty like Dad said?"

Chet's eyes went wide. "Pirate's booty? You mean like gold and jewels and stuff?"

"I doubt it," Frank said. "Why would pirates come to Bayport to hide their treasure? And why would anyone draw a map to it on an old burger wrapper instead of just digging it up?"

Chet shrugged, looking a little disappointed. "Okay, so maybe it won't be pirate booty," he said. "But I hope it's something good!"

Just then Joe stopped short. He was still out in

front. "Shh!" he hissed over his shoulder to Frank and Chet. "I hear voices."

Frank heard them now too. It sounded like a couple of people muttering to each other.

"What if someone else found our treasure?" Chet whispered, sounding worried. "Maybe that dotted line was the end of the trail instead of the beginning!"

Frank tiptoed forward. When he pushed aside some branches, he saw a clearing up ahead. Two teenage boys were standing there. One was short and wiry with a wispy, dark mustache. The other was taller and heavier with spiky hair and a silver nose ring. Frank couldn't tell for sure, but it looked like the nose ring might be shaped like a skull.

He carefully let the leaves fall back into place. "Those guys look pretty tough," he whispered to Joe and Chet. "Maybe we should hide out and wait for them to leave."

"Okay," Chet whispered, backing away.

CRACK! One of Chet's sneakers came down on a dry branch. It snapped in two, making a loud noise like a starting pistol going off.

"Hey!" a voice yelled from up ahead. "Who's there?"

"Should we run for it?" Chet whispered, sounding frantic.

But it was too late. The two teenage punks had already rushed over. They glared at the three younger boys.

"What are you doing here?" the taller one demanded. "This is our spot!"

"Yeah," the other guy added with a sneer. "Twerps not invited."

"Oh yeah?" Joe retorted boldly. "I thought this was a public park."

Frank groaned. Sometimes he wished his brother didn't have such a big mouth!

Sure enough, the teens looked angry. "Get out!" the guy with the nose ring snarled, coming at them. "Unless you want us to *make* you get out!"

"Yeah." The shorter guy grabbed at Frank's arm.

Frank twisted away just in time. "Run!" he shouted.

5

Running and Hiding

Joe could hear Chet panting loudly behind him as they raced off through the woods. Frank was in the lead. He ran down one trail and then another.

"Faster!" Chet cried, sounding terrified. "Are they catching up?"

"I don't think so." Joe slowed down, listening. "I don't hear them anymore."

He stopped. So did Frank and Chet.

"I guess they didn't want to catch us," Frank

said. "They just wanted to chase us away."

Chet looked anxious. "How are we supposed to find that treasure now? The trail starts back in that clearing!"

"I know." Joe shrugged. "Maybe we can try again after lunch. Those guys might be gone by then."

Frank nodded. "If not, we'll figure out a new plan."

"Hi, Mom!" Joe shouted. He had to shout to be heard over the noise of the vacuum cleaner.

Joe and Frank had just arrived home for lunch. Their mother was vacuuming the living room, and their father was nowhere in sight.

"Hi, boys," Mrs. Hardy said, switching off the vacuum. She grabbed a rag and started dusting the coffee table. "What are you doing home so early?"

"Early?" Frank checked his watch. "It's twelve thirty."

Mrs. Hardy looked alarmed. "Already?" she cried. "But I haven't touched the dining room yet, let alone the foyer. . . ."

She hurried off into the next room, clutching her rag and muttering to herself. Frank stared after her.

"Weird," he said. "Mom's in a total cleaning frenzy."

"Yeah. That's not like her." Joe glanced at the vacuum. "She hates cleaning." Mrs. Hardy usually left most of the vacuuming and dusting to the cleaning lady, who came once a week.

Frank was already heading toward the kitchen. "I'm starved. Let's make ourselves some sandwiches."

Soon the brothers were fixing lunch. Joe was still thinking about their mother's cleaning spree.

"I know why Mom's such a clean freak all of a sudden," he said. "Aunt Gertrude's coming tonight, remember? She's a cleaning machine. Mom probably doesn't want to hear her grumble about how dirty the house is, so she's cleaning up before her visit."

"You may be right," Frank agreed. "Mystery solved."

Joe grinned. "Except for the mystery of why Mom isn't making Dad help," he said. "After all, Aunt Gertrude is *his* sister."

Just then their mother rushed in carrying some folded dish towels. "Hey, Mom," Frank said. "Where's Dad?"

Mrs. Hardy dropped the towels on the counter. "Your father?" she mumbled, sounding distracted. "He's out doing some shopping."

She raced away again before the boys could say anything else. Joe stared at his brother.

"Did you hear that?" he asked. "Double weird.

Dad hates shopping just as much as Mom hates cleaning!"

"Maybe it's opposite day," Frank joked. "But I know one thing for sure. If we hang around too long, Mom will probably make us help her clean."

Joe's eyes widened. "You're right. Let's get out of here!"

They hurried outside with their sandwiches. Crossing the backyard, they headed into the woods.

Their tree house was invisible to anyone who didn't know it was there. But as soon as Joe tugged on a rope attached to a pulley, a ladder tumbled down. The boys climbed up into the tree house, then pulled the ladder up after them.

"Whew!" Joe flopped down onto the wooden floor. "At least we never have to clean anything up here."

Frank took a bite of his sandwich. Then he wandered over to the whiteboard hanging on the wall. The notes from their last mystery were still written there. "Guess we should start making some notes for our new mystery," he said, wiping away the old ones.

Joe liked solving mysteries, but he hated taking notes. Still, he had to admit that Frank's notes helped sometimes.

"Are you going to list the six *W*s?" he asked.

The words "Who," "What," "When," "Where," "Why," and "How" were still written down one side of the board. Frank picked up the pen and stared at them.

"I'm not sure what to write," he admitted. "We don't know much except that we're looking for treasure. We don't even know what kind of treasure it is."

He wrote "Treasure?" by the word "What."

Joe chewed a bite of sandwich. "We don't know who hid it," he said. "Or when, or even why. The only part we might be able to figure out is where and how, thanks to that map."

He pulled out the map and looked at it. This time he noticed that blob of reddish goo under the dirt. "Hey, I have an idea," he said. Brushing off some of the dirt, he tasted the goo. "We were right. It *is* ketchup." Joe licked his lips. "And it doesn't taste that old. So the map probably isn't old either."

Frank looked kind of grossed out. But he turned back to the whiteboard and wrote "Recently" beside the word "When."

"Anything else?" Frank asked, staring at the mostly blank board.

Joe took another bite of his sandwich. It was pretty good, but not as good as the ones his mom made.

"Maybe we should write up our other case," he joked. "You know—the mystery of why Mom and Dad are acting weird lately."

Frank grinned. "Good idea."

He drew a line to make a second column beside the *W* words. Next to the words "Who" and "What," he wrote "Mom & Dad" and "Acting weird." Next to the word "How," he wrote "Mom cleaning" and "Dad shopping."

"You can fill in When," Joe pointed out. "They seemed perfectly normal until the last day or so. And Where is easy too. Right here at home."

Frank scribbled all that down on the board. "The only thing we need to figure out is Why," he said.

"I think I know the answer to that one too." Joe rolled his eyes. "They're probably just acting nutty because Aunt Gertrude's coming to visit."

"I don't think that's it," Frank replied. "You're

the only one Aunt Gertrude drives nuts. Besides, she comes to dinner at least once a month, and sometimes for the weekend. Mom and Dad have never acted this way about her visits before."

"I guess you're right." Joe popped the last bite of his sandwich into his mouth. "Then I guess we really do have two mysteries to solve. But right now we'd better get back to the park so we can solve the one that might help us buy some cool new skateboarding posters for our new room over the garage!"

6

On the Trail

"I hope those jerky guys didn't find our treasure," Joe said as he and Frank walked toward the park.

"Me too." Frank was still thinking about the other mystery. "Hey, what if we're moving to a new house or something?"

Joe looked confused. "What do you mean? Do you think we'll find enough treasure to buy a whole new house?"

Frank laughed. "No, I'm talking about the *other* mystery," he explained. "What if the reason Dad fixed up the spare room and Mom is cleaning everything is because they're going to sell our house and move to a new one?"

"If that was the reason, why wouldn't they tell us?" Joe shook his head. "No, I still think they're planning some kind of surprise, like giving us the spare room."

"But why would they clean up the rest of the house for that?" Frank asked, kicking at a rock in the path.

Joe shrugged. "Okay, maybe Dad's going to have another story written about him in the newspaper," he said. "Maybe he's out buying new clothes and Mom is cleaning so everything will look extra good in the photos."

Frank thought about that. It seemed possible. Their father and his crime solving had been written up in local newspapers and magazines several times in the past.

"Could be," he said. "But I don't know why that would be a big secret either."

"Maybe they don't want to tell us until after Aunt Gertrude leaves," Joe suggested. "She's always saying Dad's work is too dangerous. What if they don't want her to know about the story, and they're afraid we might forget and say something in front of her?"

"Maybe. If that's it, I guess we'll find out after she goes home."

By now they'd reached the park. Chet was there waiting for them with Iola.

"Hi, Hardys," Iola said. "I can't wait to go treasure hunting!"

"You brought your sister?" Joe asked Chet with a frown. "Does that mean we have to split the treasure with her, too?"

Iola made a face at him. "It was my brother who found the map," she reminded Joe. "You're just lucky we're sharing with *you*!"

"Come on." Frank was already heading toward the woods. "If those punks are still hanging around, there might not be any treasure to share."

They followed the dirt trail they had started

down earlier. When they got close to the clearing, they slowed down and kept quiet.

"Do you hear anything?" Chet asked Joe.

Joe glanced back at him. "Only you yelling in my ear," he whispered back. "Be quiet or they'll hear us!"

But when they reached the edge of the clearing, there was no sign of the teens. Just a few soda cans and empty food wrappers lying around.

"What litterbugs," Iola said with a disapproving shake of her head. "Should we pick up their trash?"

"We can do that later," Frank said. He bent over the map, tracing the dotted line with one finger. It was kind of hard to see, but he was pretty sure it led into the woods on the far side of the clearing. "Come on, I think it's this way."

All four of them headed back into the trees. Frank kept his finger on the dotted line on the map, following along as they went.

"Over here," he said, ducking under a tree branch to follow a smaller trail.

"Are you sure?" Chet panted.

Frank checked the map again. "Pretty sure," he said. "Everyone watch for a creek."

"There it is!" Joe pointed to a trickling stream that crossed the trail up ahead.

Iola jumped over it. "Now what?" she asked.

"Keep going straight for a while, and keep a lookout for a big tree with a V-shaped trunk," Frank directed, peering at the map. "At least, I'm pretty sure that's what's drawn here."

"We should keep a lookout for those mean guys too," Chet added. "We don't want to run into *them* again."

"Do you think they know about the treasure?" Iola asked.

Joe shrugged. "Who knows? But if they don't, we definitely shouldn't tell them."

They walked a little farther until they spotted the V-shaped tree. It was in the middle of a small, sunny clearing. "Okay, what's next?" Joe asked his brother.

Frank checked the map. He traced the dotted line along the narrow path. Over the creek, past the V-shaped tree . . .

"Oh no!" he exclaimed as he saw where the line went next. "It goes right off the page!"

"What do you mean?" Iola grabbed the map to look. Then she gasped. "He's right!" she cried. "The end of the trail is on the part of the map that's chewed off. It's a dead end!"

7

Follow Your Nose

But we've got to find that treasure!" Joe looked around in dismay. "How much farther could it be? We should just start digging!"

"Are you kidding?" Iola handed the map back to Frank. "We can't dig up the whole forest. That's crazy. Let's forget about the stupid treasure and go back and see if anyone wants to play dodgeball."

Chet was gazing at the ground. "I could try looking for tracks," he said. "Maybe I can trace the steps of whoever hid that treasure."

"Hey, that's a good idea!" Frank said.

Joe and Iola both turned to stare at him. Even Chet looked surprised.

"Huh?" Joe said. "You mean you really think Chet can follow tracks to the treasure?"

Iola shook her head. "Get real. He's only even been into tracking for like a day and a half." Then she glanced at her brother. "No offense."

Chet just shrugged.

Frank was grinning. "No, not Chet," he said. "But I think I know of someone who maybe *can* track down that treasure."

"You do?" Joe asked. "Who?"

"Come on." Frank turned back down the trail. "I'll show you."

"What do you want with Biff, anyway?" Phil asked Frank.

"Yeah," Joe put in. "Who's Biff, and how's he going to help us find that treasure?"

Frank smiled as he walked along the sidewalk near Phil's house with his friends. He still hadn't told anybody his plan. First he needed Phil to show them the way to Biff's house.

"Biff's that really tall kid who goes to the other elementary school," he told his brother, Chet, and Iola.

"Yeah," Phil said. "I know him from soccer camp. He's cool. But what's this about a treasure?"

Chet quickly explained about the map. "But the part with the final hiding spot got chewed off by an animal or something, so we didn't find the treasure," he finished.

Joe nodded. "And I still don't get how this Biff kid is going to help us do it," he complained.

"Not unless he's the one who chewed off the corner," Iola said with a giggle.

Frank laughed. "I don't think so," he said. "But anyway, it's not really Biff we need." His eyes lit up as they turned the corner. In a yard up ahead a tall, blond kid their age was playing with a lively puppy. "It's *him*!" He pointed to the puppy.

Joe's eyes lit up. "That's a bloodhound!" he cried. "Of course! I should have remembered."

That was Frank's plan. Like Joe, he'd seen Phil's friend walking his new dog around town the past week or so. He also remembered his father talking about how a bloodhound had helped him solve one of his cases by using its super-sensitive nose to track down a missing person. Now Frank was hoping Biff's bloodhound could follow his nose to the treasure, even if they couldn't follow the map.

Biff heard them talking and wandered over. "Hi, Phil," he said, tugging on the leash as the puppy jumped around. "What's up?"

"To be honest, I'm not sure," Phil said. Then he introduced Biff to Frank, Joe, Iola, and Chet. "They all go to school with me," Phil explained. "I think they might need your help. Or Chuck's help, anyway."

Biff glanced down at the puppy. "His name

isn't Chuck anymore," he said with a sigh. "I just can't decide what to call him. None of the names I think of seem right."

Frank wasn't too interested in the puppy's name. He was much more interested in what the puppy could do. "Does your bloodhound know how to track yet?" he asked eagerly. "Because we have a mystery we need him to help us solve."

Biff looked interested. "I don't know," he said. "My mom says he tracked down the dog treats she tried to hide in a drawer. So I guess he does know how to follow his nose. What kind of mystery?"

Taking turns, they all told Biff about the map. By the time they finished, he was just as excited as they were.

"I can't believe there might be a real hidden treasure right here in Bayport!" he exclaimed. "That's awesome!"

"So you'll help us?" Chet asked.

Biff grinned. "Sure. Come on, boy," he told the puppy. "Let's go!"

Soon they were all back in the woods. Frank led the way to the little clearing where they'd lost the trail.

"See if he can sniff around and pick up any kind of trail," Joe told Biff.

Iola was patting the bloodhound puppy. "I think you should call him Nosy," she said. "He definitely likes to follow his nose."

"Nosy?" Chet wrinkled his own nose. "That's a dumb name."

"Over here, boy." Biff pulled Nosy—or Chuck—or whatever-his-name-was—over to the spot Frank had pointed out. "Find that treasure!"

Nosy-Chuck-Whoever barked, seeming just as excited about the search as the rest of them. Maybe *too* excited. He raced around in circles, sniffing at anything and everything. When a squirrel rustled in the underbrush, he leaped at it so fast that he almost pulled Biff down.

"Settle down, boy!" Joe exclaimed. "Otherwise we'll have to name you Hyperdog!"

Biff laughed. "That's a pretty good name for him."

"Keep trying to get him to find the trail," Frank urged. "Maybe he just needs a minute to settle down."

Biff kept trying. But it was no use. The puppy was just too active. Every time he put his head down to sniff something, another scent captured his attention. He ended up mostly running around in circles.

Finally Frank sighed. His great idea wasn't turning out to be so great after all. "Maybe we can find a grown-up bloodhound somewhere," he said. "Do you know of any, Biff?"

Before Biff could answer, Chet let out a cry. He was poking around near the edges of the clearing.

"What is it?" Phil asked him.

Chet looked excited. "I just spotted some tracks over here," he said. "They're leading away in the direction the trail was going. Do you think whoever made the map might've left them?"

The others raced over. Sure enough, several human footprints led out to the far side of the clearing.

"Whoa!" Joe said. "Good work, Chet."

Iola looked surprised. "I can't believe your tracking stuff actually worked," she told her brother.

At that moment the puppy let out a loud, happy bark. He jumped ahead so fast that Biff lost hold of the leash.

"Hey, come back!" Biff cried, rushing after the puppy.

But the puppy stopped just a few steps beyond the clearing. He wagged his tail and jumped up on someone standing in the woods. It was Adam Ackerman!

8

A New Lead

What are you doing lurking out there?" Joe demanded, rushing over and grabbing the puppy's leash.

Adam sneered at him. "It's a free country. I can stand wherever I want."

"Were you spying on us?" Frank asked.

"So what if I was?" Adam looked around as the others caught up. "It's not like you were doing anything interesting."

Joe and Frank traded a worried look. How much had Adam heard?

At least he won't dare try to grab the map or anything like that, Joe thought. *Adam might be a big bully, but he's not stupid enough to face down six other kids at once.*

Still, Joe knew it wasn't going to be easy to continue their search as long as Adam was hanging around. How were they going to get rid of him?

"Go away," Iola told Adam with a frown.

Adam folded his arms over his chest and leaned back against a tree. "Who's going to make me?" he taunted. "You and your loser brother?"

"Hey, watch it," Biff said. He took a step forward. He was even bigger than Adam.

That made Adam shut up. But it didn't make him leave.

Suddenly Joe had an idea. He leaned closer to Frank. "Just play along," he whispered.

Frank looked confused. But he nodded.

Then Joe grabbed the puppy's leash off the ground. "Whatever, Adam," he said loudly. "Just don't get in our way, okay? This dog is a tracking machine, so it's not like you have any chance of finding the treasure before us."

"Treasure?" Adam stood up straight. "So that's what you nerds have been doing out here?"

"It's ours, okay?" Joe exclaimed. "So don't even bother to follow us because you're not getting any of it!"

With that, he turned and raced off into the woods. He was careful to go in the opposite direction of the real trail. The puppy ran along with him, letting out an excited bark.

"That's right, boy!" Joe yelled. "Follow your nose to the treasure!"

Then he sneaked a peek over his shoulder. Biff had followed a few steps, looking confused. But Frank was whispering something in his ear.

Adam was the only one running after Joe. "It's a free country!" he shouted. "I can go anywhere I want, and you guys can't stop me."

Joe didn't answer. He just ran faster. "Find the treasure, boy!" he called out.

After that he and the puppy led Adam on a twisting trail through the woods. Luckily, Adam didn't seem to notice that the others weren't following.

Finally they reached a clearing behind a row of houses. Someone had made a big trash dump there. The middle of the clearing was piled high with cardboard boxes, spoiled food, old mattresses, and all kinds of other junk.

"Is this it, boy? Right here under this pile?" Joe said loudly, giving the puppy a pat. "Good work!"

Then he looked back at Adam. This was going to be the tricky part. . . .

Joe pasted a nervous expression on his face. "Oh," he said. "I guess you're the only one who kept up, huh?" He peered over Adam's shoulder, pretending to look for the others.

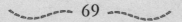

Adam grinned. "Yeah," he said, pushing past Joe. "And you know what they say. Finders keepers! Now scram and let me find my treasure!"

Adam clenched his fists and made a threatening face. Joe backed away, pretending to be scared. "O-okay," he said. "But only until my friends get here! Then you'd better watch out!"

Adam smirked. "They'll have to hurry if they want to stop me from finding the treasure."

He hurried over to the trash pile. Kicking aside an aluminum can, he started to dig through the pile.

Joe wished he could stay and watch. It would be pretty funny to see mean Adam Ackerman covered in garbage. But he had more important things to do.

Giving a tug on the puppy's leash, he headed back into the woods.

• • • •

By the time Joe and the puppy made their way back to the others, Chet had tracked the footsteps another twenty yards down the trail.

"Hurry up!" Iola called when she spotted Joe. "I think we're getting warmer!"

Chet pointed to another footprint. "This way!" he cried.

For the next few minutes the trail was clear. Joe felt his heart pounding with excitement as he clutched the puppy's leash. They were going to find the treasure!

But then the trail crossed a gravel path. On the far side was an open, grassy meadow with just a few gnarled old trees in it. And no matter how hard Chet looked, he couldn't find any more footprints.

"Man!" Phil said with a frown. "I thought we had it."

Frank sighed. "Me too."

Joe's shoulders slumped. Could it be true? Had they really reached another dead end?

Then he felt the puppy tug on the leash. With a bark, the young bloodhound jumped forward. He put his nose to the ground and sniffed. Then he sniffed again. Then he let out a deeper, louder bark and took off toward one of the gnarled trees.

"I think he's got a scent!" Biff said, hurrying after him.

"Probably just another stupid squirrel," Iola grumbled. But she followed the puppy too. So did the others.

The puppy reached the tree. He started dancing around it, howling happily.

"Do you think the treasure's buried under this tree?" Chet asked.

Joe had another idea. He'd just spotted a knot in the trunk. Stepping forward, he reached inside.

"Hey! There's something in here!" he cried.

He pulled out a plastic shopping bag. When he looked inside, he gasped. It was full of cash!

"We're rich!" he yelled.

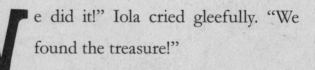

9

Cash Back

We did it!" Iola cried gleefully. "We found the treasure!"

"Your puppy's awesome, Biff!" Chet exclaimed, grabbing the little bloodhound and giving him a hug.

"Yeah, he's a real detective," Joe agreed. "Hey! That gives me a great idea. You should call him Sherlock! You know, like the famous detective Sherlock Holmes."

Iola laughed. "That's cute! My dad loves those books."

"Sherlock, huh?" Biff grinned and bent down to ruffle the puppy's fur. "What do you think? Huh, Sherlock?"

The puppy barked. Everyone laughed.

"I think he likes it," Phil said. He was counting

the money from the bag. "Wow, there's a ton of cash in here! Oh, and some gum and candy and stuff too."

"Cool," Chet said eagerly. "How much will we each get if we divide the money six ways?"

Frank gulped. He was starting to feel uneasy about this. "Wait a minute," he said, reaching for the bag of cash. "It looks like this bag is from the KwikSnak. You know, the convenience store on Third Street."

"So what?" Iola said.

"So, what if this money belongs to the store?" Frank said. "If it does, we can't just keep it. It wouldn't be right."

Joe bit his lip. For a second he looked ready to argue. But then he sighed. "Maybe you're right," he muttered.

Phil nodded. "We should at least check it out."

The others looked disappointed, but they all nodded too. "It's not like finding the booty of old-time pirates or something," Chet said. "If this belongs to a real living person right here in Bayport, we need to return it."

Frank was glad that they all agreed. The mystery of figuring out the rightful owner of the cash wasn't as exciting a mystery as following that treasure map. But it was even more important.

"Hello, Mr. Bersal," Frank said when they reached the front of the line at the KwikSnak. As usual for a Saturday afternoon, the store was busy. "Sorry to bother you. We were just wondering if your store, um, got robbed anytime lately?"

The cheerful store owner frowned. "As a matter of fact, Frank, yes!" he exclaimed. "Just a couple of days ago. Some teenage punks came in looking for a certain kind of soda. One of the kids had a nose ring. Millie was working that afternoon, and when she went to the back to see if we had the soda,

the kid grabbed all the cash out of the register and took off!" He shook his head. "Ah, what's Bayport coming to these days?"

"We have good news, Mr. B," Joe said. "We think we might have found your money."

Phil held up the bag. Mr. Bersal gasped as he looked inside.

"I can't believe it!" he cried. "Where did you get this?"

"We found it in a hollow tree out in the woods behind the park," Chet said.

"Yeah," Iola added. "And Sherlock helped!"

Mr. Bersal looked kind of confused by that. But he also looked happy. In fact, he was beaming from ear to ear.

"Thank you so much!" he exclaimed. "You kids are real heroes!"

10

Secret File #3:
Two Cases Closed

An hour later the Hardys were back in their tree house. Frank was writing on the whiteboard while Joe counted a handful of cash.

"Awesome!" Joe said as he shoved the money back into his pocket. "It was really nice of Mr. Bersal to give us all a reward!"

The convenience store owner had been so pleased to get his money back that he'd immediately counted out a nice reward for all six of the kids. He'd also grabbed a box of dog treats off a shelf for

Sherlock. He'd even offered each of the kids their choice of a piece of candy from beside the register. Frank had put away his chocolate bar for later. But Joe was already sucking on the blueberry lollipop he'd picked.

"I know," Frank said. "He didn't have to do that."

Joe grinned around his lollipop. "Nope. But I'm glad he did!"

The reward wasn't as much as if they'd split the money they'd found. But Joe didn't mind. Somehow, it felt even better knowing they'd helped someone. No wonder their dad loved his job so much!

"Now we can fill in the whole W list," Frank said as he went back to writing. "We know who did it. It was those two punks we saw in the clearing."

Joe nodded. Mr. Bersal had called the police, and they'd found the teens right away. They were still lurking around out in the woods. It turned out they had been in Bayport after visiting some relatives in a neighboring town. That was why neither Mr. Bersal nor the kids knew who they were. The teens admitted to the robbery and explained that they'd made the map so that they'd remember where the money was—but when they came back to Bayport after their visit, they realized they'd lost the map!

"I bet those guys never come back to Bayport again," Joe said.

Frank was still focused on the whiteboard. "What—stealing the money from the KwikSnak," he murmured as he wrote. "When—this past Thursday. Where—the KwikSnak. Why—because they're greedy. How—by hiding the money in a tree trunk."

He finished writing and stepped back. The board looked much better with everything filled in.

Joe wasn't paying much attention. He was trying to decide what to buy with his reward money.

"I might get that new video game Phil was telling us about the other day," he mused, slurping on his lollipop. "Then again, maybe I'll wait. I might need the money to decorate my new room over the garage."

Frank rolled his eyes. "I keep telling you . . . ," he began.

But he broke off as he heard his mother's voice in the distance. She was calling their names, and she sounded kind of anxious.

Frank looked at his watch. "Uh-oh," he said. "It's later than I thought. We're late to meet Aunt Gertrude!"

Joe groaned.

Frank poked him in the shoulder. "Hurry up!"

He normally wouldn't mind Aunt Gertrude's visit at all. She was always nice to him. But today he couldn't help feeling a little impatient. He and Joe hadn't had a chance to tell their father about solving the mystery yet, since Mr. Hardy had been off picking up Aunt Gertrude at the train station by the time they got home. And now they'd have to wait even longer.

"We probably shouldn't say anything about the treasure and stuff while Aunt Gertrude is here," Frank told Joe as they climbed down the rope ladder.

"Yeah," Joe mumbled around his lollipop. "She probably wouldn't like to hear that we're following Dad into the detective biz."

When they got inside, their parents were standing in the front hall with Aunt Gertrude. There was a big stack of boxes and suitcases piled just inside the door. Joe was so surprised that he almost spit out his lollipop.

"What's all that stuff?" he blurted out.

"Hello, Frank," Aunt Gertrude said in her crisp, no-nonsense voice. "You're looking well. Joe, what's that you're sucking on?"

She reached out and plucked the lollipop right out of his mouth. Joe was too startled to protest. Besides, he knew it wouldn't do any good.

"Surprise!" Mr. Hardy sang out, beaming at them and waving a hand at the luggage. "Aunt Gertrude is coming to live with us!"

"What?" Frank said.

Joe was too astounded to say anything.

Mrs. Hardy looked amused. "I told you they'd be surprised, Gertrude."

The adults went on to explain that Aunt Gertrude was getting tired of city life. Mr. and Mrs. Hardy had invited her to come live with them in Bayport. At first she'd refused, saying she didn't want to be a burden. But Mr. Hardy had started fixing up the spare room just in case she changed her mind. And finally she'd agreed to give it a try.

"But only under the condition that I make myself useful around the house," she told the boys.

Mrs. Hardy smiled at that. Joe could guess why. His mother was probably hoping that this weekend's cleaning spree had been her last!

Joe shot Frank a look. So now they knew what all the secrecy was about. He couldn't help feeling disappointed. It sounded as if he and Frank were stuck sharing their old room after all.

"So what do you think?" Mrs. Hardy asked the

boys cheerfully. "It will be fun having your aunt around full-time, won't it?"

"Sure," Frank said with a smile.

Aunt Gertrude patted him on the shoulder. "I'm looking forward to helping you with all the interesting school projects you're always telling me about, Frank," she said. Then she glanced at Joe. "As for you, young man, one of my duties will be making sure you do *much* better in science class this year." She held up the half-eaten lollipop she was holding and frowned at it. "And that you stop eating so much candy."

Joe smiled weakly.

As the whole family trooped into the dining room, Frank leaned closer to Joe. "Guess we're not such great detectives as we thought," he whispered. "We never saw this one coming."

Joe nodded. "Not only am I not getting my own cool new room over the garage," he whispered back,

"but I'm also going to have to move out to the tree house full-time to get away from Aunt Gertrude's boot camp!"

Frank shrugged and smiled. "It won't be so bad."

Joe didn't answer. He just slumped into his seat at the dining table.

Aunt Gertrude was sitting across from him. "Elbows off the table, young man," she warned.

Joe snapped to attention. "Nope, definitely boot camp," he muttered to Frank, who was sitting beside him. "Case closed!"